BIGFOOT

AND OTHER STRANGE BEASTS

by Rob Shone

illustrated by Nick Spender

The Rosen Publishing Group, Inc., New York

Published in 2006 by The Rosen Publishing Group, Inc.
29 East 21st Street, New York, NY 10010

First edition, 2006

Designed and produced by
David West Books

Editor: Charlotte Cattermole

Library of Congress Cataloging-in-Publication Data

Shone, Rob.
  Bigfoot and other strange beasts / by Rob Shone ; illustrated by
Nick Spender.
  p. cm. -- (Graphic mysteries)
  Includes bibliographical references.
  ISBN 1-4042-0793-7 (lib. binding) -- ISBN 1-4042-0804-6 (pbk.) --
ISBN 1-4042-6260-1 (6 pack)
  1. Sasquatch--Juvenile literature. 2. Yeti--Juvenile literature. 3.
Wild men--Juvenile literature. I. Spender, Nick, ill. II. Title. III. Series.

  QL89.2.S2S56 2005
  001.944--dc22

                                                          2005017604

Manufactured in China

CONTENTS

BIGFOOT TYPES

No one has ever managed to capture a Bigfoot. Yet many eyewitness reports and lots of physical evidence from countries all over the world have been collected. These suggest that a large unknown ape may exist, but it can take several different forms...

BIGFOOT – This creature takes its name from the huge footprints that it leaves behind. Bigfoot has been sighted mainly in North America, usually in mountainous forest regions. It is human shaped, but much larger and with longer arms, and is apelike in appearance.

What is claimed to be a female Bigfoot was filmed in Willow Creek, California, in 1967. It is undecided whether or not the footage is genuine.

YETI – The Yeti lives in the Himalayan regions of Southern Asia. Its color varies from white to dark reddish brown.

YEREN – Yeren is the Chinese name for "Wildman." Thought to be a giant ape species hunted to extinction thousands of years ago, this creature may still exist in the mountains of China. Scientists think there is a big and smaller version.

KAKI BESAR – Kaki Besar is Malaysia's version of Bigfoot. Sightings have been reported of a giant hairy creature in the jungle.

Could Bigfoot be a hominid, and so be an extension of the human species? Drawings such as this one of an early hominid point to a resemblance between humans and Bigfoot.

ALMA – Sightings of this creature are similar to Bigfoot reports. However, the Alma is said to look more like the type of human known as Neanderthal, than like apes. These beings are thought to live in the Caucasus Mountains in Asia, formerly a part of the Soviet Union.

FLORIDA SKUNK APE – This Bigfoot is said to live in Florida. Its name comes from the awful smell that it gives off. It is believed to be seven feet tall.

YOWIE – There are two different types of Yowie that have reportedly been seen in Australia. Sightings date back hundreds of years to when Native Australians told of such creatures living in the forests.

ORANG-PENDEK – Sumatra's Wildman is a short ape that walks on two feet. It is similar to an orangutan, but walks upright all of the time, not just for a few steps.

This photograph is thought by some to be of a Florida Skunk Ape. It was sent to a Florida sheriff's office.

THE WILD WORLD

From small tribes in central Asia to campers in the United States, stories about creatures like Bigfoot and the Yeti have come from all the continents on Earth.

BIGFOOT HAUNTS

Rumors and sightings of huge apelike creatures in the Pacific Northwest date to the arrival of early settlers to the region. However, the first detailed account of Bigfoot was in 1811, when an explorer discovered large footprints near the Rocky Mountains in Canada. The area's Native Americans, who greatly respect Bigfoot, told the explorer that the tracks belonged to Sasquatch. Since then, other reports have come from all over the vast lands of North America, from Canada in the far north, to California in the south.

There have been many Bigfoot sightings in the Rocky Mountains in Canada and on the northwest coast of North America.

Beijing

N
W   E
S

Fang Xian
HUBEI
Shennongjia
Forest

TIBET   CHINA

HIMALAYA MOUNTAINS

NEPAL   Mt. Everest

INDIA

The dramatic scenery of China is home to many rare and unusual animals. Does it also hold the Yeren?

THE BAMBOO FOREST OF CHINA

The Hubei Province of central China is rich in legends and stories. It is still a relatively unknown and mysterious place. There are references from 2,000 years ago to the existence of strange apelike creatures, sometimes called "Mountain Ogres." Ancient Chinese poets even wrote about such animals.

THE YETI'S ICY HOME

The name "Yeti" is another term for "abominable snowman." This is because reports of the creature nearly all occur in the snowy regions of the Himalaya mountains in Tibet. Yeti sightings have come from many sources, including experienced mountaineers and sherpas.

The white mountain slopes of the Himalayas may make it easier to spot a dark-furred Yeti. But they have also been seen in the thick forests that grow beneath the snowline.

THE YETI

THE HIMALAYA MOUNTAINS, NEPAL, 1959.

HOW MUCH FARTHER? THERE'S A STORM ON THE WAY.

LOOK!

THERE'S THE MONASTERY! COME ON!

PRAYER FLAGS! WE ARE CLOSE.

INSIDE THE MONASTERY'S WALLS...

WELCOME. I AM THE MONASTERY'S ABBOT. WE DO NOT GET MANY VISITORS TO THIS REMOTE PLACE.

HI, MY NAME IS PETER BYRNE.

WHAT BRINGS YOU ALL THIS WAY?

I WORK FOR AN AMERICAN OIL COMPANY. WE WERE CHARTING THE AREA WHEN THE STORM BLEW IN.

WE KNEW YOUR MONASTERY WAS NEARBY, SO HERE WE ARE.

LET US GO INSIDE WHERE IT IS WARM.

WE WERE TOLD SOME STRANGE THINGS WHILE WE WERE DOWN IN THE VALLEY. TALES OF UNEXPLAINED MURDERS.

YES. NEWS OF THE CRIMES HAS REACHED US.

THE VILLAGERS ARE BLAMING SOME KIND OF MONSTER. THEY CALL IT THE YETI. THEY SEEM TO THINK YOU'RE AN EXPERT ON THE MATTER.

TELL ME WHAT YOU HAVE HEARD.

AT EACH VILLAGE THE STORY WAS THE SAME...

SURELY YOU DON'T THINK THERE'S A MONSTER LOOSE IN THE MOUNTAINS? THE ATTACKS COULD HAVE BEEN MADE BY A BEAR, OR EVEN BANDITS.

THE MOUNTAINS HAVE SECRETS, MR. BYRNE. PEOPLE HAVE SEEN THINGS THAT ARE HARD TO EXPLAIN. LET ME TELL YOU COLONEL HOWARD-BURY'S STRANGE STORY...

IN 1921, COLONEL HOWARD-BURY LED A BRITISH EXPEDITION TO CLIMB MOUNT EVEREST.

THE CLIMBERS HAD BEEN MAKING GOOD PROGRESS.

SUDDENLY, HIGH ABOVE THEM ON A SNOWFIELD...

LOOK! UP THERE! SOMETHING'S MOVING!

WHO IS IT? THERE ARE NO OTHER CLIMBERS IN THE AREA!

COULDN'T IT HAVE BEEN A SHELTER THAT THE LOCAL YAK HERDERS USED?

POSSIBLY. BUT LET ME TELL YOU CAPTAIN D'AUVERGNE'S STRANGE TALE. IT WAS 1938. THE CAPTAIN HAD GONE WALKING IN THE MOUNTAINS, ALONE...

...A BLIZZARD STRUCK AND...

...THE CAPTAIN BECAME LOST.

HE FELL, SNOW-BLIND AND EXHAUSTED.

HE AWOKE TO FIND HE WAS SAFELY OUT OF THE STORM. FOOD HAD BEEN LEFT FOR HIM.

THE CAPTAIN STAYED IN THE CAVE UNTIL HIS STRENGTH AND EYESIGHT RETURNED.

IF HE WAS SNOW-BLIND, HOW DID HE KNOW WHAT HAD SAVED HIM? NO, ABBOT, I'M STILL NOT CONVINCED THERE'S ANY SUCH THING AS A YETI.

COME WITH ME. I WISH TO SHOW YOU SOMETHING.

THESE ARE RARELY SHOWN TO OUTSIDERS. THEY HAVE BEEN AT THE MONASTERY FOR CENTURIES. THEY ARE BELIEVED TO BE HOLY.

THE RELICS! TOM SLICK WAS RIGHT, THEY **ARE** HERE!

THE SCALP AND THE HAND BONES OF A YETI.

MY EMPLOYER, MR. SLICK, IS A KEEN COLLECTOR OF UNUSUAL ITEMS LIKE THESE. HE WOULD...

HE'S A TEXAS MILLIONAIRE. HE'LL PAY WHATEVER YOU ASK.

MR. BYRNE, THE RELICS ARE **NOT** FOR SALE!

THE RELICS MUST NEVER LEAVE THIS MONASTERY.

BY MORNING THE STORM WILL HAVE DIED DOWN...

THE STOLEN YETI BONES WERE SNEAKED BACK TO LONDON. THERE THEY WERE SEEN BY DR. W.C. OSMAN-HILL. AT FIRST HE SAID THEY WERE HUMAN.

LATER, HE CHANGED HIS MIND, SAYING THEY WERE NOT QUITE HUMAN. SHORTLY AFTER, THE BONES DISAPPEARED - AND HAVE NOT BEEN SEEN SINCE.

THE END

THE WILDMAN OF CHINA

BEEEPP!
BEEEPP!

BEEEPP!

ARE YOU ALRIGHT?

I THINK SO.

18

WHO IS HE? IS HE IMPORTANT?

YES. HE'S A SCIENCE PROFESSOR FROM BEIJING.

YOU KNOW HIM?

HE'S MY BOSS. AND I'M LATE FOR WORK! HERE, BUY SOME NEW VEGETABLES.

THANKS!

THE HEADQUARTERS OF THE SHENNONGJIA FOREST YEREN EXPEDITION...

AH! DOCTOR ZHOU, COME IN. I READ YOUR EXPEDITION REPORT. IT'S NOT BAD. IT'S A PITY YOU DIDN'T FIND A WILDMAN, THOUGH.

PROFESSOR.

I DON'T KNOW IF WE SHOULD CARRY ON WITH THIS RESEARCH, DOCTOR. IT COSTS MONEY, AND WITHOUT A WILDMAN TO SHOW FOR IT... WELL, IT'S HARD TO SEE WHY WE SHOULD CONTINUE.

WE DID FIND NEW EVIDENCE, PROFESSOR! FOOTPRINTS, DROPPINGS, AND LOOK—HAIR.

AND SOME OF THE EYEWITNESS REPORTS ARE GOOD TOO. THE FIREWOOD GATHERERS FROM SHENNONGJIA—THEIR STORY IS VERY STRONG.

THE FIREWOOD COLLECTORS? YOU'LL HAVE TO REMIND ME...

THOCKKK!

LIAO CONGGUI AND HIS NEPHEW WERE GATHERING FIREWOOD IN THE SHENNONGJIA FOREST.

THIS FOG'S GETTING THICKER. NEPHEW, KEEP CALLING OUT SO I KNOW WHERE YOU ARE.

I CAN HARDLY SEE A THING NOW...

WHERE ARE YOU? SHOUT OUT!

GRUNT!

STOP PLAYING GAMES, LAD! I DON'T SCARE **THAT** EASILY!

GRUNT! GRUNT!

GRUNT!

SNAPP!

HUH?!

WHO'S THERE?

YES. A BELIEVABLE STORY, BUT...

I HAVE SUPERIORS, TOO, DOCTOR. THEY ONLY WANT TO KNOW WHEN THEY CAN SEE A YEREN IN A CAGE.

IF THEY STOP THE RESEARCH, THAT MAY NEVER HAPPEN.

AND WE DID COME SO CLOSE TO SUCCESS...

THE 1977 EXPEDITION TO THE SHENNONGJIA FOREST HAD BEEN ONE OF THE LARGEST OF ITS KIND. IT WAS DUE TO LAST ALMOST ONE YEAR. AS WELL AS SEARCHING FOR THE YEREN, THE SCIENTISTS ALSO STUDIED THE FOREST'S PLANT AND ANIMAL LIFE.

WITH THE SCIENTISTS WERE HUNTERS WITH TRANQUILIZER DARTS, SCOUTS, AND SOLDIERS. IN ALL, MORE THAN 100 PEOPLE WERE INVOLVED. DOCTOR ZHOU WAS THE HEAD OF A SPECIALIZED GROUP THAT TRAVELED DEEP INTO THE HEART OF THE FOREST-COVERED MOUNTAINS.

CAN YOU SEE IT? IS IT MOVING, DOCTOR ZHOU?

IT'S JUST SITTING THERE. I DON'T THINK IT'S A BEAR.

MAYBE THE EXPEDITION WAS TOO BIG. DOZENS OF PEOPLE CRASHING THROUGH THE UNDERGROWTH WOULD HAVE SCARED EVERYTHING AWAY.

DO YOU BELIEVE YEREN EXIST, DOCTOR?

SOMETHING BIG IS OUT THERE.

HERE, LET ME READ YOU AN ACCOUNT OF THE FANG XIAN INCIDENT, PROFESSOR...

MAY 14, 1976. NEAR FANG XIAN, HUBEI PROVINCE...

A GROUP OF GOVERNMENT OFFICIALS WERE RETURNING HOME AFTER ATTENDING A MEETING.

SUDDENLY...

SLOW DOWN! LOOK!

BIGFOOT

WELL, ALL WE NEED NOW IS TO FIND THIS THING'S BODY AND TAKE ITS PICTURE. YOU'VE GIVEN ME A GOOD STORY, FRED...

LET ME READ BACK WHAT YOU'VE TOLD ME SO FAR. STOP ME IF I'VE GOT ANYTHING WRONG...AHEM! IN JULY OF THIS YEAR, 1924...

...FRED BECK AND FOUR FRIENDS SET OFF FOR MOUNT ST. HELENS, IN WASHINGTON STATE.

THEIR GOLD MINE, THE VANDER WHITE CLAIM, WAS TWO MILES EAST OF THE MOUNTAIN.

THERE'S THE CABIN. THE MINE'S A LITTLE WAY UP THAT HILL.

THE PROSPECTORS SETTLED INTO THEIR NEW HOME.

WHEN YOU BUILT THIS PLACE, DIDN'T YOU THINK TO ADD WINDOWS, PETE?

THE CABIN WAS NOT ONLY HOME TO THE MINERS...

RATS! I HATE THEM!

HOLD A LIGHT OVER THAT SACK OF POTATOES, FRED.

BLAMMM!

SQUEEKKK!

PETE, IT'S A GOOD THING YOU CAN SHOOT STRAIGHT. BECAUSE...

THIS ISN'T A POTATO...

?!!

THERE'S ENOUGH DYNAMITE IN THIS POTATO SACK TO BLOW US ALL CLEAN OFF THE MOUNTAINSIDE!

OVER THE NEXT FEW DAYS, THE MINERS STARTED WORKING THEIR CLAIM, USING THEIR MUSCLES...

...AND THEIR DYNAMITE TO FIND THE GOLD SEAM.

BOOOMMM!

BUT IT WAS NOT LONG BEFORE THE MEN REALIZED THAT SOMETHING WAS WRONG.

SCREEECHHH!

DID YOU HEAR THAT, FRANK?

I HEARD IT YESTERDAY, TOO.

WHAT IS IT?

I DON'T KNOW. IT DOESN'T SOUND LIKE ANY ANIMAL THAT I'VE EVER HEARD BEFORE.

THE STRANGE SOUNDS CONTINUED. THE MEN WENT AROUND ARMED AT ALL TIMES.

I'M GOING DOWN TO THE STREAM TO FETCH SOME WATER, FRED. WANT TO COME?

WELL, SURE FRANK.

BRING YOUR RIFLE.

THEY DECIDED TO TURN IN FOR THE NIGHT. THEY PLANNED TO PACK UP AND LEAVE AT SUNRISE...

MIDNIGHT...

BANG!

UH?

KERRRBANG!

BANG!

CLANNNG!

GET UP! SOMEONE'S THROWING ROCKS AT THE CABIN!

THE ROCKS HAD KNOCKED AWAY SOME OF THE MORTAR BETWEEN THE LOG WALLS OF THE WINDOWLESS CABIN.

THERE'S SOMETHING MOVING AROUND OUT THERE!

WELL I'LL BE...! IT SEEMS LIKE THERE'S THREE OF THEM, BUT THEY DON'T LOOK...HUMAN!

THEY'RE ON THE ROOF!

KLUMP KLU

THE MEN LOADED THEIR CAR.

WHAT ABOUT ALL OUR MINING GEAR? IT'S WORTH HUNDREDS OF DOLLARS.

STAY AND GUARD IT IF YOU LIKE, JOE.

LOOK!

OVER THERE!

ROARRRR!

THE FOUR MINERS LEFT AS QUICKLY AS THEY COULD...

BACK IN THE NEARBY TOWN, KELSO, THE MINERS' STORY SPREADS...

READ ALL ABOUT IT! APEMEN ATTACK MINERS!

APEMAN ATTACK!

FRED, I'M TELLING YOU. THIS WHOLE TOWN'S GONE APEMAN CRAZY!

PEOPLE FROM ALL OVER THE COUNTRY ARE TURNING UP HERE, WANTING TO SHOOT ONE OF THESE MOUNTAIN DEVILS. SEE THAT GUY OVER THERE? HE'S COME ALL THE WAY FROM ENGLAND! HE OWNS THE BIGGEST RIFLE I'VE EVER SEEN. HE MUST THINK WE'VE GOT ELEPHANTS ROAMING THE WOODS!

THE PLACE IS CRAWLING WITH NEWSPAPERMEN, TOO. A REPORTER FROM PORTLAND WANTS ME TO SHOW HIM THE CABIN AND MAYBE FIND THE DEAD APEMAN...

FRED AND THE REPORTER REACHED THE BOTTOM OF THE CLIFF...

...AND THAT'S AS FAR AS I'VE GOT. NOW, WHERE'S THIS DEAD APE?

IT SHOULD HAVE LANDED AROUND HERE SOMEWHERE.

FACT OR FICTION?

Are these accounts of large, hairy creatures actually sightings of Bigfoot? Do the many tracks and footprints found come from Bigfoot beasts or just wild animals?

Casts of footprints like these have helped to make Bigfoot world news.

IS THERE ANYTHING OUT THERE? Taken together, the thousands of sightings of Bigfoot creatures indicate that this is a matter that requires careful study. They have encouraged scientists to look more closely at these cases.

FOOTPRINTS IN THE SNOW It is possible that tracks in the snow, such as those found by the explorer Eric Shipton in 1951, were made by the local people of the Himalayas, who can walk on snow without shoes.

Could there be large animals hidden away, still waiting to be found? The African mountain gorilla was not seen by Western explorers until 1902.

CAUGHT ON CAMERA

Filmed sightings of Bigfoot creatures are rare. Roger Patterson's Willow Creek footage, shot in California (see page 4), is the best to date. It has divided people into those who believe it is real and those who think it is someone dressed in a costume.

A SCIENTIFIC APPROACH

Many scientists are doubtful about the existence of Bigfoot, as there is not enough solid evidence. But with the discovery in recent years of many new and large animals, they are starting to accept that Bigfoot might be another creature waiting to be found.

Scientists are now testing the DNA in hair samples to see whether they could belong to Bigfoot. The genetic tests will see if they match up to human or ape hair, or to the hair of any other species.

HOAXES

Some people have admitted, after several years of keeping their secret, that they lied about their sightings and made up evidence. Ray L. Wallace said that he had created the famous Bigfoot tracks found in California in 1958.

The possible existence of "apemen" has fascinated us for centuries. This picture was drawn in the sixteenth century.

GLOSSARY

abbot The senior monk in a monastery.

claim Something that one declares ownership over, such as a plot of land.

embankment The raised edge of something, mainly a river, road, or railway.

extinction No longer existing.

genuine The real thing.

Himalaya mountains The world's highest mountain range. It is in Asia and covers Nepal, Tibet, India, Pakistan, and Bhutan.

holy Spiritually pure, godly, or sacred.

hominid Member of the species that humans belong to.

incident A specific event.

Kathmandu The capital city of Nepal.

lair The home of a wild animal.

monastery A place that is home to a community of religious people who eat, live, pray, and worship together.

monk A male member of a religious community.

mortar A mixture of cement, sand, and water that is used in buildings to join bricks.

Neanderthals One of the earliest forms of human on Earth.

Nepalese Mountains Part of the Himalaya range, it has fourteen of the world's highest mountains.

prospector Someone who explores an area, usually for minerals.

relic An object that has been preserved and is highly thought of.

remote Somewhere that is far away from anything else.

research An investigation or examination of something, and the information uncovered by such an investigation.

Sasquatch A name for Bigfoot used by several Native American tribes of the Pacific Northwest.

semester One of two terms in the academic year.

shaman A healer heavily influenced by spiritual beliefs.

Sherpa An expert guide of the Himalaya mountains.

snow-blind When sunlight reflects off the snow causing pain and sensitivity to light in the eyes.

superstitious To be influenced by a fear of the unknown or the supernatural.

tranquilizer A drug used to induce sleep.

undergrowth Shrubs and bushes that grow in a forest.

yak A long-haired ox from Tibet.

FOR MORE INFORMATION

ORGANIZATIONS

Bigfoot Discovery Museum
5497 Highway 9
Felton, CA 95018
(831) 335-4478
Web site: http://www.bigfootdiscoveryproject.com

Willow Creek-China Flat Museum
P.O. Box 102
Willow Creek, CA 95573
(916) 629-2653

FOR FURTHER READING

Carmichael, Carrie. *Bigfoot: Man, Monster, or Myth?* Orlando, FL:
Steck-Vaughn, 1977.

Gaffron, Norma. *Bigfoot: Opposing Viewpoints (Great Mysteries).*
Chicago, IL: Greenhaven Press, 1988.

Gorman, Jacqueline Laks. *Bigfoot (X Science: An Imagination
Library Series).* Milwaukee, WI: Gareth Stevens Publishing, 2002.

Levy, Joel. *K.I.S.S. Guide to the Unexplained.* London: Dorling
Kindersley Limited, 2002.

Miller, Heather. *Bigfoot (Monsters).* Chicago, IL: KidHaven
Press, 2005.

Owens, L.L. *Bigfoot: The Legend Lives On.* Des Moines, IA:
Perfection Learning, 1999.

INDEX

Web Sites

Due to the changing nature of Internet links, the Rosen Publishing Group, Inc., has developed an online list of Web sites related to the subject of this book. This site is updated regularly. Please use this link to access the list:

http://www.rosenlinks.com/grmy/bosb